The Reluctant Mole

and More Beastly Tales

The Reluctant Mole

and More Beastly Tales

Philip Welsh

Illustrated by Fred Apps

Scripture Union

© Text Philip Welsh 1979—The Reluctant Mole and Other Beastly Tales
© Text Philip Welsh 1984—Ignatius Goes Fishing and More Beastly Tales
© Illustrations Scripture Union 1979, 1984
The stories 'Hercules the Secret Service Flea' and 'It's not much Fun being a
Slug' first appeared in the magazine *Together,* published by the Church of
England Board of Education.

First published as combined edition 2001
Reprinted 2002
© Text Philip Welsh 2001
© Illustrations Scripture Union 2001

Scriptrue Union, 207—209 Queensway, Bletchley, Milton Keynes, MK2 2EB,
England

Email: info@scriptureunion.org.uk
Website: www.scriptureunion.org.uk

ISBN 1 85999 496 2

British Library Cataloguing-in-Publication Data.
A catalogue record for this book is available from the British Library.

Printed and bound in Great Britain by Ebenezer Baylis and Son Ltd., The
Trinity Press, Worcester.

Scripture Union ia an international Christian charity working with churches in
more than 130 countries, providing resources to bring the good news about
Jesus Christ to children, young people and families and to encourage them to
develop spiritually through the Bible and prayer.

As well as our network of volunteers, staff and associates who run holidays,
church-based events and school Christian groups, we produce a wide range
of publications and support those who use our resources through training
programmes.

To my children
Margaret and Michael

Dear Readers,

Years ago I used to miss my breakfast quite often on Tuesday mornings, because right up until ten to nine I was stabbing away at my typewriter with two fingers, getting a story ready to tell at assembly to the children and teachers at the school attached to my church.

Without a scrap of pity for my poor fingers, getting shorter by the week, the children kept asking for more. I suppose it was because the stories were set in a world we could all recognise, because that was where we all lived: a world of old houses split into flats, of chip shops and bike sheds and of the legendary 65 bus, which has only ever been seen by a handful of people.

Once these stories were published, with terrific pictures by Fred Apps, I'd get letters from complete strangers demanding to know if there would be more. By then, I'd moved to a new church, but to my surprise all the animals came with me, and like me began to make new friends. Soon another series of adventures came out.

Now the two sets of stories have been brought together in one book. I've moved around a bit since I last supervised the Grand Old Malden Quadrupeds' Marathon Race, but I'm told that the animals are still up to their old tricks. We can learn a thing or two from what they get up to, but best of all they are a lot of fun. I hope you enjoy getting to know them.

Philip Welsh

Contents

ARFA THE DISGUSTING CAMEL

Just along the main road past the church there used to be
an enormous house. It could have been a really good
house, but it wasn't. The rooms were gloomy, paint was
peeling off the walls, and all around the house was a tall thick
hedge, that nobody ever cut. To make it worse, it was a grey
hedge because of all the traffic dust. Arfa the Camel lived there,
by himself. He didn't care about the house. He was a
disgusting, miserable creature. That's why they'd called him
Arfa. As soon as he was born, they took one look at him and
said, 'Yuk! This isn't 'arf a disgusting camel.'

Arfa had just one friend, though he didn't treat him very
well, and his name was Frank. One day Frank came round to
see him. He went to bang the door knocker, but then he
remembered that it had come off years ago, and Arfa had never
bothered to fix it. So he rattled a few dirty milk bottles, until
Arfa came shuffling to the door.

'Hello, Arfa,' he said, when eventually the miserable creature
opened up. 'Oh,' Arfa replied, 'it's you. Well, I suppose you
had better come in.' So in they went, to the damp and dreary
parlour.

'Tell me, Arfa,' said Frank, 'why are you looking even more

11

Mrs Grady was
so surprised she
dropped her shopping
all over the pavement

miserable and disgusting than usual today? Your hump's all crooked, you haven't polished your hoofs, you haven't even combed your hairy ears.' 'Why should I bother?' said Arfa. 'Nobody ever comes to see me, the rotten lot. They just don't understand what a fascinating and charming and altogether special creature I am.'

At this point Frank suddenly had to pretend to blow his nose, so he could cover his face with a huge red spotted handkerchief. You see, he didn't want Arfa to see him laughing. He knew that people like Arfa, who take themselves so seriously, can never see the funny side of themselves. And Arfa took himself very seriously.

'You know what your trouble is?' said Frank. 'You want everyone to love you first. Only if they say what a splendid fellow you are, will you ever be friendly to them. But if you really want to know how to make people like you, I'll tell you the trick. Don't stand around waiting for them to notice how special you are. Go out and pretend they're special too.'

'Oh,' said Arfa, scratching his ear in a puzzled kind of way. 'Well, we'll see.' Frank had got him thinking now, but he didn't want to say so.

When he went out to the shops next day, he met his next door neighbour, Mrs Grady. The two of them hadn't spoken to each other for months, because Arfa didn't think she showed the proper respect that a very special camel like him ought to receive. So he lifted his great black nose right up in the air, bristled his hairy ears, and got ready to walk straight past her as if she didn't exist. But then he suddenly remembered the trick that Frank had told him the day before. 'Let's see if it works,' Arfa said to himself, 'I'll pretend she's special, like me, and see what happens.'

'Good morning, dear Mrs Grady,' he said in a cheerful voice. 'How very nice to see you.' She was so surprised she dropped her shopping all over the pavement. 'Let me give you a hand, or rather a hoof,' said Arfa, chasing a tin of beans as it rolled towards the kerb. 'You must be worn out carrying that lot.'

'Well, thank you, Arfa dear,' she replied, 'I'm glad I met you. Why don't you come to tea this afternoon?'

'My goodness!' said Arfa to himself. 'She called me "dear" – the trick works, just like Frank said!' So off he ran, as fast as his four knobbly legs could gallop, to the yard where Frank worked. 'It works!' he shrieked, as he clattered to a standstill. 'It's magic! I pretended she was special just like me, and she called me "dear" and invited me to tea.' 'Of course it works, you daft camel!' said Frank, chuckling away, 'But it's not magic. Everyone *is* special underneath, just like you. But if you spend all your time thinking how very important only you are, you never notice how special everyone else is, too. The secret is, to treat other people the way you'd like them to treat you. And don't wait for them to make the first move.'

Lord Jesus, you taught us to treat other people the way we would like to be treated ourselves. Help us to remember that we are all special in your sight.

ARNOLD THE 'ARD-UP AARDVARK

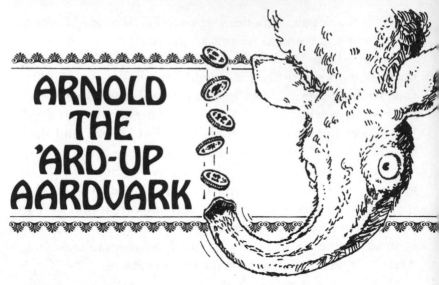

J ust over the wall at the back of St Andrew's church is a house with a large garden. And in the garden, right up against the church wall, is a broken down old shed with a leaky roof. In this shed there lived a most peculiar animal. His name was Arnold, and Arnold was an aardvark.

An aardvark is a long, brown, dirty, rather soggy-looking animal, with very short legs, very tiny eyes and a great long, pointed nose. He uses this to dig up his favourite food, which is ants.

Our particular aardvark had one problem. He was very poor. That's why he lived in a shed. And that's why they called him Arnold the 'ard-up Aardvark. 'If only I was rich!' he would think, 'Then I could have boxes of special chocolate-covered ants flown in from Switzerland.' What made him really fed-up with being poor was that nobody wanted to have anything much to do with him.

One sunny day, Arnold was sniffing his way along the garden, looking for fat juicy ants, when all of a sudden his long, pointed nose bent up against a huge, black, shiny, military boot. And who should be on the other end of the boot, sitting in a deckchair, than Arnold's miserable neighbour, a retired army major, who lived in a flat right at the top of the house.

Like a lot of army officers, he had a double-barrelled name. His mother's name was Miss Feele until she married, and his father's name was Mr Gloomy. So he called himself Major Feele-Gloomy, which was a good name, because that's just what he did: he made you feel gloomy.

'Out of my sight, despicable aardvark!' roared Major Feele-Gloomy, 'I know your type. You're just a scrounger who can't be bothered to make a living. I ought to know. I was hard up once. But I pulled myself together, and became the man I am today.'

'It's all right for you,' thought Arnold to himself, 'I bet you had important friends to help you out. What am I supposed to do?'

So annoyed was Major Feele-Gloomy to meet Arnold the 'ard-up Aardvark, that with one great kick of his huge, black, shiny, military boot he sent him flying over the wall, right into the churchyard.

Arnold flew
over the wall,
right into
the churchyard.

Seeing he'd ended up at the church, Arnold thought he'd call
on his one friend, a little creature who was, like him, as poor as
a church mouse. In fact, he *was* a church mouse. He was called
Ignatius, which was a very holy name for a not very holy
mouse. Arnold went round to the church door, but he was too
short to reach the handle, so he wormed his way in through a
ventilator, and found Ignatius busily chewing up the notice
board.

'Where on earth did you get that boot-shaped dent in the
side of your head?' asked the mouse. So Arnold told him. 'You
do know, don't you,' Ignatius said as he bandaged Arnold's
head, 'why Major Feele-Gloomy kicked you over the wall like
that? He didn't want to be reminded just how many poor
people there are in the world. Just because he was lucky
enough to get out of being hard-up himself once, he thinks it's
easy for everyone.'

'Is everyone like him?' Arnold asked in a bleak little voice.
'I'm afraid quite a lot of them are,' replied Ignatius. 'But I'll tell

you one thing. When I'm here on a Sunday during the services, I'm usually too busy biting the choirboys' ankles to listen to much. But now and again, when I've had enough of this, I listen to some of those things they say about Jesus. And it strikes me that Jesus had quite a soft spot for anyone who was hard-up, like you and me. If they were down on their luck, or poor, or the kind of people nobody wanted to know, then Jesus made particular friends of them. It was the rich people, who didn't want to bother about anyone else, that he was angry with.' As Arnold limped back to his draughty shed, he thought about what Ignatius the church mouse had told him. He hoped that one day, if he was lucky enough to be comfortable and not to get kicked around, he wouldn't forget about all the people who were still hard-up.

Heavenly Father, help us not to turn away from those in need. Teach us that wherever we help someone in trouble, it is as if we were helping you.

HAROLD THE RELUCTANT MOLE

Everyone in Surbiton knew Harold the Mole, because he'd lived in the same place for years, in a hole in the garden of St Andrew's church. No one could ever budge him from this rather scruffy hole, even though he'd grown too fat for it, and could only squeeze in by holding his breath and flattening his ears. 'Why should I move?' he said, 'I've got used to it here. I feel at home and safe.'

One day Harold was inside his hole, whistling to himself, as moles do, and frying for his tea a couple of juicy antburgers. Suddenly there was a scratching noise, and down into the hole came a large brown envelope. On the front, in important looking writing, it said: 'Harold, Esquire, Mole Hole, St Andrew's Garden.' It was from the Mole Housing Association, and inside it said: 'Dear Mole, we are sorry to tell you that we are filling in all the holes in your area, and must ask you to move. We will be glad to give you a brand new council molehole in a new estate the other side of Chessington.' Harold collapsed, thunderstruck, on to his sofa. He'd always been in this hole. He couldn't imagine moving, and having to leave all his old friends, and the streets and the gardens he'd always lived in. He'd never known anything else. To be honest, Harold was very frightened. So he did a stupid thing. When the other animals asked him about his move, he always said, 'Oh yes, of course I'm looking forward to it.' He wouldn't own up to being frightened, but kept pretending to be cheerful. The result was he felt even worse, because he couldn't tell anyone how worried he was. Only he knew – at least, that's what he thought. In fact, the other animals soon saw he was pretending. People always do. They wished they knew how to help him.

The day before he was due to move house, Harold invited his best friends to tea in the garden. He spent all morning buying them the things they liked to eat best: coconuts for Arfa the camel, chocolate-covered ants for Arnold the aardvaark, and hymn-books for Ignatius the church mouse. But all the time he was shopping he was thinking, 'Oh dear! Oh dear! This is the last time I shall be able to give my friends tea like this! Oh dear!' And of course, instead of enjoying the thought of having a party he just made himself more and more miserable. Finally, just as they all sat down to tea, Harold burst into tears. He couldn't pretend any longer. 'Oh, I don't want to go,' he wailed, 'I don't know anyone the other side of Chessington. I'll never see you all again.'

'Of course you will,' said Arfa, 'we've only got to hop on the 65 bus, and we can come and see you. And you can come back here on the bus to see us as often as you like. So instead of bumping into each other at the shops, like we do now, it'll be a special occasion.'

'That's right,' said Arnold, 'I felt just like you before I came to live here. Everyone gets a bit frightened when they have to go somewhere new. That's because you have to leave your old friends before you get the chance to make new friends. But as soon as you do, you feel much better.'

'I can remember, ' piped up Ignatius, who was a bit younger than the others, 'when I had to leave the school for young mice I went to, and go up to the big school. When I thought of going to that huge new place, I got quite upset. But it wasn't half as bad as I thought. After a couple of days, I felt I'd been there for years.'

Harold
collapsed,
thunderstruck,
on to his
sofa.

They could see Harold was beginning to cheer up. It all seemed much less frightening now. So as soon as tea was finished, Harold put on their favourite record, 'The Moles' Tango', and they all got up and danced and leaped about. When they were too tired to dance any more, they got out the Scrabble. When they were too tired even for Scrabble, they talked and talked and talked until the stars came out; and long past their bedtime, they wandered home. 'See you next Tuesday, then,' they shouted as they left Harold. 'We'll come out on the 65 about tea-time, to inspect your new place.' 'Righto,' said Harold. And although he didn't say so, he was beginning to look forward to moving.

Heavenly Father, help us when we are frightened because we have to go somewhere new and leave our old friends for a while.

HARVEY THE SKATEBOARDING OCTOPUS

arvey wanted a skateboard very badly. But skateboards cost a lot of money. To make it worse, Harvey had to have three skateboards, because he was an octopus. If he had three skateboards, he could put two legs on each skateboard, and still have two legs left over to wave around in the air. But however was he going to get the money for three skateboards? His mum and dad said that whatever pocket money he saved up, they'd give him the same amount again. So he started to work it out: 'If one skateboard costs me £20, and I need three skateboards, and I save 10p pocket money a week, and mum and dad give me the same amount of money again, it will take me . . . mmm . . . almost six years. Oh dear.' His heart sank down to his boots. All eight of his boots. He stared out of the window, and there, going past on their new skateboards, were his friends from along the street. 'Six years!' he thought. 'There must be another way I can get some money . . .'

He looked up, and there, at one end of the mantelpiece was a neat pile of five 10p pieces. Every Thursday night his dad put them there when he came in from work, ready to give the football pools man when he called. 'He won't miss one, just one,' thought Harvey, and stretched out one of his long rubbery legs and took the top coin. When the man from the football pools came, his dad noticed that he was 10p short. He looked puzzled for a second, then got another 10p out of his pocket, and thought nothing more of it. 'Clever old me,' said

'He won't
miss just one,'
thought Harvey.

Harvey to himself, 'he never guessed!'

Next day, Harvey looked up on the mantelpiece again. There, at the other end, was another neat little pile of five 10p pieces. These were the ones his mum kept for the machines at the launderette. 'I'll just have one,' thought Harvey, and stretched out another of his long, wavy legs and picked up 10p. Just as he put it away, in came his mum with a bag of washing. 'I'm just off to the launderette, Harvey,' she said, picking up the money. 'You haven't seen the other 10p have you?' she asked. 'No,' said Harvey innocently, looking out of the window. His mum wasn't bothered though, and off she went. 'Clever old me!' he thought again, rubbing his legs together. 'If I go on like this,' thought Harvey, 'I'll soon have my three skateboards.' So the next week, he did just the same again. 'You haven't seen my football money have you?' said Harvey's dad to his mum. 'No,' she said.

'That's odd,' he went on, 'I was short last week, too.'

'How peculiar,' she said. 'My launderette money's been short as well.' They looked at each other, and they looked at Harvey, and Harvey looked as hard as he could out of the window, humming a feeble little tune, but shaking inside. They didn't say anything. They knew he'd swear blind he'd never touched the money. 'Anyway,' they thought, 'what if we're wrong, and it isn't Harvey at all? He'd feel awful if we accused him. He'd think we don't trust him.'

So they didn't say anything. But Harvey noticed that there was no more money on the mantelpiece after that. He began to feel awkward. He'd never lied like that to his parents before. He didn't like the feeling that now his mum and dad kept their money hidden away, because they were suspicious. There was something else he noticed, too. Quite often his dad used to say to him: 'Nip round the corner for me, will you son, and get a newspaper? And get yourself some sweets, too. And don't forget the change,' but he never did that now. Now when he wanted a paper, he'd say: 'I think I'll go myself tonight. I fancy some fresh air.' It was the same with Harvey's mum. She used to say to him when he got home from school: 'Oh Harvey, pop round the baker's for a loaf, will you?' But now, if she ran out of something, she'd rush round to the shop herself, even if she was in the middle of cooking.

'It wasn't meant to turn out like this,' said Harvey to himself. 'It wasn't supposed to make any difference. But it's no fun at home now they don't trust me to be honest. I wish I could own up, but I daren't.' The more he thought about it, the more worried he got. 'Come on,' said his mum that evening, 'eat your tea, Harvey.' But he couldn't. He was too miserable. 'Now then, my lad,' she said, 'what's wrong with you?' As she looked at him, he could tell what she was thinking, so he gathered all his courage together, and burst out: 'I took that money, because I thought I'd never get my skateboards otherwise. But now I wish I'd never been near the mantelpiece.' As soon as he'd said it, he shrunk back as far as he could, wrapped his eight legs around himself, and waited to feel the sting of his mother's hand as she walloped him. Nothing happened. So slowly he opened first one eye, then the other, and gradually looked up. There she was, smiling. 'What are you laughing at me for?' he said. 'Well you see, Harvey,' his mum said, 'we thought it was you all the time, and as long as you didn't own up we couldn't trust you. But now you've been brave enough to own up, we can forgive you and trust you again. That's why I'm glad. So pop round the corner to the baker's, and get yourself a cream cake. And you never know, you might not have to wait as long for your skateboards as you thought.'

Heavenly Father, help us to be honest and trustworthy, so that other people know they can rely on us.

28

HERBERT THE HEDGEHOG'S NEW SISTER

Near the bikesheds round the back of St Andrew's church, there lived a family that hardly anyone knew about, because they kept very quietly to themselves under the hedge. Which was the proper place for them, because they were hedgehogs. Mother, father, and their son who was called Herbert. Herbert liked it there, with just his mum and dad.

Except for Friday nights. Friday night was the dreaded choir practice, when the hedgehog family had to roll themselves up tight into three prickly balls, so they wouldn't get hurt when the choirboys played football with them. Instead the boys would hurt their toes. Serve them right. But apart from that, they were happy.

One day, Herbert's mother told him, with a little smile, that she was going to have a baby. Herbert didn't know what to say. He was so used to the three of them. He couldn't imagine what it would be like to have a fourth member of the family. 'But just think, Herbert,' said his mum, 'you'll have a new little brother, or maybe a sister, to look after and play with.'

'That doesn't sound too bad,' thought Herbert, and cheered up.

As the weeks went by, they all got more and more excited, though sometimes Herbert got a bit lonely, because his mum

Quick as lightning the policeman plonked his helmet on top of Herbert

had to go and lie down a lot. The strangest bit was when his mum had to go into hospital for a few days, to have the baby. It was most peculiar, and not much fun, just him and his dad on their own every night, having to live on baked beans and tinned rice pudding because they couldn't cook properly.

Then came the great day. All morning Herbert and his dad worked away to get the place tidy, throwing out all the old tins and half-eaten bits of toast. Then, in the afternoon, there was his mum again, proudly carrying in his new baby sister, Jasmine, whose prickles were just beginning to come through. Herbert was really pleased with his new sister, even though she wasn't old enough to play with yet.

After a few days, though, things began to go all wrong. Herbert got more and more fed up and prickly. Whenever he wanted his mum, she always seemed to be looking after the baby. And at tea-time, he had to wait for his tea, getting hungrier and hungrier, until the baby had been fed. Worst of all, when he wanted his parents to take him to the cinema in Kingston, to see a film that had come round at last, about a giant man-eating hedgehog called Spike, they said they had to stay in because of the baby. Herbert felt bored, and he felt left out, and he began to get into all sorts of trouble. Sometimes he would roll himself up into a tiny, hard, prickly ball, and jam himself under one of the choirboys' bikes, so that as soon as the bike started, it got a puncture. Sometimes he wouldn't come straight home from school. He'd roam the streets till after dark, looking for mischief. 'I bet they won't even notice I'm out,' he muttered. But they did notice, and they got so worried one night, that they sent for the police. So to Herbert's surprise, as he was dawdling along the road, a policeman stopped him. 'Are you Herbert the Hedgehog?' he said, from a great height. Herbert's prickles began to shiver, and he started to run. Quick as lightning, the policeman took off his helmet and put it down, plonk, on top of Herbert, before he could get away. That was how the policeman carried him home, squealing inside the dark and musty helmet.

'Where have you been?' said his mum and dad. 'We've been worried sick.'

'I didn't think you'd bother about me,' said Herbert. 'You spend all your time fussing over the baby.' Sure enough, just as he said that, the baby started wailing, and his mum rushed off to see what was wrong. 'Look', said his dad, 'I know it's not easy for you getting used to Jasmine, but I'll tell you what – you and I can go to the pictures tomorrow afternoon to see Spike the Man-eating Hedgehog.'

As they bumped along on the top of the bus next day, his dad said, 'You know, Herbert, before you were born, there were just the two of us, your mother and I. Then you came along, and your mother had to spend half her time looking after you, and I had to learn to look after myself a bit more. Otherwise you wouldn't have grown up properly. Now it's your turn to look after yourself a bit more. But don't forget that your mum loves you just as much, even though she has to look after the baby a lot at the moment.'

Herbert hadn't seen it that way before. And he was still thinking it over when his dad said. 'Come on, it's the next stop.' Soon Herbert was lost in the adventures of his hero, Spike the Man-eating Hedgehog. 'I hope this film comes round again', he said afterwards, 'then I'll be old enough to take Jasmine to see it.'

Heavenly Father, bless our homes and families, our brothers and sisters, and especially help those children who are unhappy at home.

THE TWITCHING LEATHER SOCKS

J ust as you go into St Andrew's church, on the left-hand side, there's a narrow door that is always locked. This is the door to the tower, and behind the door is a staircase littered with creepy things, like dead pigeons, covered thick with dust. Nobody ever goes up there, because it's so filthy and creepy and dark. But if any brave person were to climb up all the winding stairs, then, in the gloomiest bit of all, he would see a chilling sight. In silent rows, like old socks hung up on the line to dry, hang the bats of St Andrew's, ugly creatures that hang upside down from the rafters, wrapped up tight inside their great flappy, leathery wings.

Nobody knew they were there, until one day Ignatius, the faithful church mouse, got bored with chewing up the hymnbooks, and decided to become an explorer. 'I think I'll start,' he said to himself, 'by exploring the church tower.' So he put on his four-legged overalls and his two pairs of wellingtons, tied a red handkerchief round his head, and slowly opened the creaky door. Up and up and up he went. Dustier and dustier and dustier he got. Till at long last, puffed out, he reached the gloomiest bit of all. 'That's funny,' he thought, 'somebody's left their washing hanging out. I'd better go and pull it off. Odd-looking things,' he muttered to himself. 'They look like leather socks.' He was only a little mouse, so he took

a long run, and a mighty jump, and with all his strength sank his teeth into the leathery sock. Suddenly the sock came to life! It flapped all around him, and, with a mighty shriek, said: 'Gettoff!' Ignatius dropped to the floor in terror, and through his rattling teeth he cried, 'Have mercy on me, O sock!' bowing his little pointed head, tied up in its red handkerchief, right down to the ground.

The bat, whose name was Oliver, said, 'You miserable midget of a mouse. Couldn't you see I was fast asleep? Can't a poor bat get a bit of peace and quiet without some fool of a mouse using him for a swing? I've often spied on you from up here. I know what you get up to when no one's looking. You just chew up the hymnbooks and bite the choirboys' ankles. You're no good to anyone.' Ignatius ran for his life, down and down and down, in a cloud of dust to the bottom of the stairs, slammed the door as hard as he could and locked it with a huge key.

When Ignatius was having his tea that evening, munching a tasty piece of notice board, he was thinking to himself, 'What a cheek of that bat Oliver to say I was useless, when day and night I keep an eye on this church.' Just then, he heard footsteps in the dark. 'That's funny,' he muttered, 'the church was locked up hours ago.' He peered through the gloom, and there he saw a burglar. 'Right,' said the church mouse, 'to work!' He got out a piece of sandpaper he always kept handy, sharpened his teeth till they were like needles, crept up behind the burglar and took a great bite into his ankle.

The burglar was in agony, but he couldn't shout out, or he'd be discovered. He had a spanner in his hand, so, quick as a flash, he stuck it into his mouth. Ignatius bit him again. This time the burglar nearly swallowed the spanner. He couldn't stand any more. In a terrible panic, he clambered through the nearest window and fell on to the pavement. As soon as he sat up, ready to run off, down swooped Oliver the bat, and whacked him across the face with his great flappy, leathery wings.

It was then that Oliver spotted Ignatius the mouse, who had

followed the burglar out and was getting ready for another bite. 'What are you doing here, you useless object?' he hissed, while he kept on whacking the burglar. 'I don't see why I should tell you,' said Ignatius, 'but it so happens that every evening I patrol round the inside of the church to make sure everything's all right, and it was me who drove the burglar out.'

'I see,' said Oliver, slowly, thinking that maybe there was more to this mouse than met the eye. Then Ignatius spoke up, 'What about you, then, you leathery horror? Why aren't you hanging around up the tower, dozing your life away as usual?'

'It so happens,' Oliver replied, 'that I sleep all day, then at night I get up when everyone else is in bed, and patrol around outside the church, keeping an eye on everything so that the birds can have a sleep. It's not the sort of thing I usually tell people, any more than you told me what you get up to.' Ignatius knew what he meant. If you do something to help, you don't go boasting to everyone. So he said to the bat, 'It looks like we've both seen the wrong side of each other, doesn't it?'

Just at that moment a policeman came around the corner. He stopped, he rubbed his eyes, but there on the pavement large as life was a burglar, wriggling and thrashing about with a spanner in his mouth, while a mouse chewed his ankle, and a bat whacked him across the face with his flappy wings. When Ignatius and Oliver saw the policeman they gave a parting bite and whack each to the burglar and disappeared into the shadows. The policeman rubbed his eyes again, and then he remembered his duty. He hauled the burglar away. No one was bothered by that burglar again for a long time.

'Come on, Oliver,' said Ignatius, when they had gone. 'I'll show you the cupboard where I live, and make us some cocoa.' 'Righto,' said the bat. And from that day on they were the best of friends. Which all goes to show, that you often don't know how much good other people get up to, because the best people do it quietly, and don't boast about it.

Heavenly Father, help us to remember how much good people do without talking about it. Help us not to boast about the things we do.

NORMAN THE HARVEST BANANA

Norman the banana was lying on his back in the sunshine one day, in a wooden box outside the greengrocer's, lazing away with a bunch of his friends.

All of a sudden, as he was lying there, turning nice and yellow, the sky was blotted out by the great hairy hand of the greengrocer coming down to grab him. 'Here we go,' Norman said to himself. 'Someone's gone and bought me.' Off he went, deep down in a shopping bag, bumping along the street, with no idea where he was heading.

After a while he dropped off to sleep. When he came round, a few hours later, he couldn't work out what was going on. Instead of waking up in a chilly glass fruit bowl as he expected, there he was, nestling in a little box full of fruit and vegetables, and being made as comfortable as possible. 'This is the life,' he thought, pinching his thick yellow skin to make sure he wasn't dreaming.

A small hand came down and picked the box up, and Norman could feel himself swaying gently along the road, together with the friendly and good-looking crowd of fruit and veg. who were sharing his box. Suddenly, when he saw where he was going, his heart sank. It was the school. 'What a fate for a high-class banana like me,' he muttered, 'to end up in a school dinner.'

But no sooner had he arrived and got his breath back, than there he was out in the fresh air again, in a long procession of children carrying other boxes and packets. 'I have a feeling,' he thought, 'that today's going to be a special day.' Just then, instead of looking up at the sky, he found he was looking up into the high wooden roof of a huge building. He was inside the church. Next – he could hardly believe it – he found himself going right up the middle of the church, where he was laid down alongside a splendid collection of fruit and vegetables, tins and jars and packets, ready for the school's Harvest Festival service. This was more like it!

But at the end of the service, his heart sank again. After the children had gone back to school, some of the mums came and shut him in a tiny room, along with all the other food. 'This is worse than prison,' he said to the great marrow who was lying on top of him. 'Don't worry,' said the marrow, 'just wait till tomorrow.' Sure enough, on the next day the people from the church unlocked all the fruit and vegetables and tins, and used them to decorate the church for their own Harvest Festival, when it was their turn to thank God for all the good things he provides. 'I've never felt so handsome before,' thought Norman, as he stretched himself on a window-ledge between a tin of pilchards and a very fat pumpkin.

On the Sunday they had the church Harvest Festival service, and there was Norman, gleaming away on his window-ledge. And they sang the same hymn that the school sang – *We plough the fields and scatter*.

'I'm fed up with all these hymns about cornfields,' thought Norman. So he sang to himself a song about bananas:
'We plough the fields and scatter
Bananas in the ground,
And next year when we come back
There'll be palm trees all around.'

When the church people had gone home, Norman had a moment of horror. He saw that the choirboys were coming to collect up all the fruit. 'Oh no!' he thought. 'What a fate for a high class banana like me! To be eaten by a choir boy!' Though to his surprise, they didn't eat him. They shut him up in the tiny room again.

All night long the fruit and tins and vegetables muttered away, wondering what was going to become of them. Then, the next day, they were all put in boxes again and carried off. 'Where are you off to?' said Norman to his new friend the marrow. 'I'm off to the hospital,' the marrow replied. 'and I'm off to the old people's home,' piped up an apple. ' 'Bye then, old fruit,' said Norman, and off he went to the house of a little old lady who couldn't get out much now.

Norman had never been more pleased than when he saw her face as she opened the door. She wasn't looking happy just because she liked bananas, but because someone had remembered her and thought to bring round some of the harvest gifts. 'It's all been worth it,' thought Norman, 'all those journeys up and down the road, and those nights shut up in the tiny room.'

But he'd never have done it at all, if somebody hadn't thought to bring him along to school as a 'thank you' to God for all his gifts in the harvest.

Thank you, heavenly Father, for all the good things you provide for us to eat. Help us to show our thanks by remembering those in need.

THE ELEPHANT AND FLEA'S TEA PARTY

Surbiton is a very popular place for retired elephants. In fact, when you see builders at work in an old house, the chances are they're strengthening the floorboards ready for yet another elephant who's grown too old for the circus, and decided it's time to hang up his trunk and settle down.

Henry the elephant lived just round the corner from the church. Like a lot of people from show business, when he retired he settled down with someone else from the entertainment world. His friend's name was Archie, and Archie was a performing flea. He used to work in a flea circus that was about the size of a biscuit tin.

When these two moved in together, nobody around could understand how on earth they managed to get on. The trouble was, Henry the elephant never forgot. He never forgot if someone was rude to him, and he never forgot if they didn't apologise. All the same, he didn't remember so well if he'd been rude to someone else.

One fine day Henry woke up, uncurled his trunk, stretched his ears and declared, 'Archie, today's my 103rd birthday, and we're going to have an elephant and flea's tea party for all the animals. So get out your address book, and we'll write the invitations. Then you can buzz off and deliver them.' Archie

opened up his tiny flea's address book at the first page —A.
'Arfa the camel,' he said. 'Oh no, we don't want him,' said
Henry. 'I can remember that last year, when it was his birthday,
he never even invited me.' 'But you were on holiday,' Archie
protested. 'That's not the point,' Henry replied, 'he still should
have invited me. I haven't forgotten that.' So Archie looked at
the next name in the book: 'Arnold the aardvark,' he read out.
'Not a chance,' said Henry. 'He put out his long sticky tongue
at me last week, and he still hasn't said he's sorry. I won't
forget that.' On they went to the next name in the book,
Harold the mole. 'Do you know,' said Henry, 'once when I
asked him to do me a favour he told me to go back to the
jungle? I still haven't forgotten. I'm blowed if he's coming.'
    So on they went, right through Archie's address book. At
the end, Henry asked, 'How many's that we've got, then?'
    'Just you and me,' the flea replied. Henry was furious, and let
out a mighty trumpeting you could hear from one end of Maple
Road to the other. 'What a miserable lot of so-called friends
I've got!' he hooted. 'They've all let me down. It's a good job I
never forget!'
    'Don't you?' said Archie, in as fierce a voice as a flea can
manage. This surprised Henry. 'What do you mean, Flea?' he
said sharply. 'Well,' said Archie, 'What about the time you
sucked me up your trunk and blew me out of the window. You
may have thought it was a great joke, but I didn't. I bet you've
forgotten that. Can't you see, Henry, you dozy great elephant,
that you're no better than all the other animals?
    'You do things that upset other people the same as they do,
only you never forget. But you've got to forgive and forget, or
nobody would have any friends left at all. That's why we've got
no one to come to your hundred and third birthday party.'
    'Hmmm,' muttered Henry, from somewhere deep in his
trunk. He didn't like the sound of this one bit. But finally he
plucked up his courage and said: 'All right, flea, you win. I can
see now that I remembered everyone else's mistakes, but forgot
all about my own. I'll tell you what I'll do. We'll get your

'What do you mean, Flea?' he said sharply.

address book out again, and I'll invite all the animals, and we'll see how it turns out.'

Never did a flea move so fast as Archie that afternoon, buzzing round all the animals with the invitations to their elephant and flea's tea party. It turned out to be a terrific party, and ended up with Henry giving them all a dizzy ride round the block on his back. From that day on, Henry, the elephant who never forgot, learned how to forgive and forget because he had found out how much he needed other people to forgive him too, and the animals still haven't stopped talking about the elephant and flea's tea party.

Heavenly Father, we know that we need other people to forgive us when we are hurtful. Teach us not to bear grudges when people are unkind to us, but to learn to forgive one another.

EVIL WEEVIL AND THE NEW SCHOOL BANNER

L ate one night inside the dark church, Ignatius, the church mouse was doing his rounds, making sure everything was locked up before he had his supper – a nice bit of toasted hymnbook. As he peered through the gloom, he saw a shape that hadn't been there before. Quietly as he could, he crept closer, and, to his surprise, he found a brand-new banner. 'What's this?' he muttered, and then he remembered. It was left over from the school service that morning, when it had been dedicated. They'd forgotten to take it home. So Ignatius ran up the pole of the banner, had a good look, and decided he'd better keep a special eye on it.

Half an hour later, after he'd finished his hymnbook, and was just looking forward to a nice bit of cushion and custard, he thought he could hear a strange scuffling noise. So he sat in the dark, and listened, and there it was again, the faint sound of hundreds and hundreds of tiny feet. Then he saw them,

thousands of them, creeping out from the plug-hole in the font at the back of the church. He realised at once who they were – they were those vicious little insects called weevils, that worm their way into everything and eat it. As they marched in a great long line two by two, he could see that these were the nastiest of all the weevils – the dreaded banner-eating weevils – and at the front was their leader, Evil Weevil.

They were heading for the banner. What could Ignatius do? 'I know,' he thought, 'I'll rush up the tower and wake up Oliver the bat.' So up he ran, ploughing his way through the inch-thick dust, and clambering over the dead pigeons, till at last he found Oliver, hanging upside down like a pair of leather socks. 'Wake up!' shouted Ignatius, poking the bat until his wings creaked and with a yawn he said: 'What's up?'

'Come quick!' said Ignatius, 'the weevils are after the school banner that was dedicated this morning.' 'Dedicated?' said Oliver. 'What does "dedicated" mean? How can I help you if I don't know what you mean by such long words?' Ignatius was getting desperate. Through a crack in the floorboards he could see that already the weevils were halfway to the banner. He only had a few minutes to save it. Now he could hear them singing the dreaded Weevils' Chewing Song:

'Give us a penny
Give us a tanner
Give us a chance
And we'll chew up your banner.'

How could he quickly explain to Oliver what 'dedicated' meant? 'I'll tell you what,' he said. 'It means that the banner isn't just any old flag. It's to remind the children that they belong to St Andrew's and St Mark's school, and to help them to be loyal to their school.'

'Oh,' said Oliver, rather dimly. 'Is it only flags that get dedicated?'

'Oh no,' said Ignatius, 'This whole church here is dedicated to God. That means that it's not just any old building, but is meant to remind everybody that they belong to God, and so

ought to be loyal to God, by doing the things that Jesus said.'
'Ah yes, I've got it now,' said the bat. 'Well, there's no time to
lose. Run down as quick as you can, Ignatius, and get hold of a
dustpan. Don't ask why, just get it.'

You never saw a mouse run so fast. He found the dustpan,
which was four times as big as he was, and went and stood in
the gap between the banner and the army of weevils,
wondering what to do as they got nearer and nearer. Then he
spotted Oliver, right at the back of the church. 'What's he
doing down there?' he thought, but he soon found out.
Suddenly, with a great clattering of his leathery wings, Oliver
swept down the middle of the church, and as he flew along, so
with his great wings he swept up the weevils and pushed them
all into the dustpan. Then Ignatius ran out the back with his
dustpan and threw them all in the dustbin. So the banner was
rescued!

By this time the sky was just beginning to get light, so
Ignatius and Oliver took the banner, and carried it along Maple
Road back to the school, much to the surprise of the early
morning paperboys and girls. And they were so sleepy after
their night's adventures that when the school caretaker
unlocked in the morning, there they were, banner and all,
asleep on the doorstep. As soon as they saw the caretaker, they
left the banner and ran away. But Oliver had one last look.
Now he knew it wasn't just any old banner, but was to remind
the children they belonged to the school. And when he got
back to the church, he looked up and thought that it wasn't just
any old building, but was there to remind people that they
belonged to God. But now it was time for school to begin, so
Oliver and Ignatius went to bed.

**Lord Jesus, please bless the work of all churches,
especially those near our home. Help all those people who
work telling others about you, and help us to be loyal to
you.**

IGNATIUS GOES FISHING

Most people don't know that our church mouse, Ignatius, is mad about fishing. Every Saturday, when he's finished sweeping the leaves out of the church porch, he gets his fishing rod out of its hiding place up the tower, puts on his wellingtons and an old fishing hat, and goes down to the river. There he sits all day, staring at the water, and often doesn't come home till the football comes on television.

One Saturday when he was there, sitting absolutely still on the bank, with ten packets of crisps still unopened at his side, all of a rush up galloped Arfa the camel.

'Oh Ignatius,' he said, as he clattered to a standstill, 'I don't know what to do. The Council's offered me a new house, but it's miles away, and I've got to go and see it this afternoon. Can you come with me? I need some help.'

"Fraid not, old man,' said the mouse. 'Any other time I'd love to come, but I'm in the middle of fishing now.' So Arfa went away.

Later that afternoon, when there were only five packets of crisps left, Ignatius suddenly saw a peculiar shape in the water coming towards him. 'My goodness,' he thought, 'It must be the cassock 'n' onion flavouring in the crisps, going to my head.'

To his amazement, out of the river came his old friend Harvey

the Octopus. 'Oh Ignatius,' said Harvey as he dripped all over the crisps, 'I'm so glad I've caught you. My mum's tied herself in a knot and I don't know what to do. Can you come and help?'

'What a pity,' said the mouse. 'Any other time I'd be round like a shot. But right now I'm busy fishing.' So Harvey went away.

As the sun was going down, and Ignatius had just one soggy bag of curry 'n' woodworm crisps left, there came through the gloom a long, pointed, furry nose, and just behind it Harold the Mole. 'I thought I'd find you here,' he said. 'I'm feeling a bit fed up tonight on my own, so I thought I'd see if you fancied some cocoa and a couple of juicy antburgers.'

'Oh dear,' said the mouse, 'it'll have to be another night, I'm afraid. As soon as I've finished fishing I've got to get back and see the big match.' So Harold went away.

When it got to ten to ten, Ignatius packed up his fishing rods and ran back to see the match. He hadn't caught a single fish. Served him right.

Next morning, Ignatius was patrolling as usual underneath the bench where the choirboys sat, trying to decide which ankle to bite first. Suddenly he heard the magic word 'fishing'. He stopped and listened, and it was a story about two brothers who went fishing one day. When they were in the middle of their fishing, up came Jesus and said to them, 'Can you come with me? I need your help.' And straight away they dropped everything and went with him.

Ignatius felt dreadful. He remembered the day before, and how his three friends had asked him to help them, but he'd just carried on fishing. So the following Saturday he made an astounding decision. He decided not to go fishing, but instead to go and see the people he'd let down the week before. He'd remember now to help people when they asked for help, not when he felt like it.

Heavenly Father, make us ready to help other people, not just when we feel like it, but when they ask for our help.

THE REVENGE OF JASPER THE TOAD

Opposite the church there were two small houses with two very different gardens. The first garden was full of long grass, and in the grass lived a rather elegant fellow called Godfrey the Grasshopper, who liked nothing better than to sway about on top of a tall piece of grass, chirping, as grasshoppers do.

The second garden was full of mud, and in the middle of the mud there lay a large and dirty pond. This was the home of Jasper the Toad, and he liked nothing better than to flop around in the mud all day, croaking so loudly it made the pond shiver.

The odd thing was, though Godfrey and Jasper couldn't have been more different, they were the best of friends, because they'd always lived next door to each other and had grown up together. Every Sunday afternoon they'd have a race to see who could hop to the church and back faster. Whoever lost had to listen to the other one singing.

But as they got older, bit by bit they saw less of each other. Godfrey was very clever. He passed all his exams at school and got a job in an office, hopping off to the train every morning looking very important.

Jasper was no good at exams. He was always bottom of the class. But he was brilliant at fixing things. Every Saturday morning you'd see his bony toad's legs sticking out from under somebody's car, that he was fixing for them. In the end he got a job at the local garage as a mechanic, and you could always find him by looking for a car that was croaking.

By this time, sad to say, Godfrey and Jasper hardly saw each other at all. Then one day, Godfrey was hopping his elegant way home from the station, with his shiny briefcase on one arm, his neatly rolled umbrella on the other arm and a tiny bowler hat on his head, not looking where he was going. Just ahead of him, lying as usual under a car engine, was Jasper, with his lanky toad's legs stretching right across the pavement.

With a horrible shriek, Godfrey tripped over the legs and went flying. His briefcase burst open, and papers from work went all over the road.

'You idiot toad, Jasper,' he hissed, mad with rage. 'If you didn't waste your time messing about with stupid cars, you wouldn't get in the way of people like me.'

Jasper wasn't going to take this lying down. 'Just who do you think you are, Godfrey?' he shouted back, waving an oily fist at the grasshopper. 'Why don't you do a real day's work for once, and get your hands dirty, instead of fiddling about with bits of paper in a boring old office?'

They both went off angrily into their gardens, and from that day on they didn't speak a word to each other.

Months later, when Godfrey arrived at work one morning, there on his desk was a letter from head office. 'We want to give you a better job,' it said. 'Come to head office at once. A car will be waiting for you downstairs.'

Full of excitement, Godfrey rushed down and found a huge, sleek car, complete with chauffeur. Off he went, feeling *very* pleased with himself.

When they were half way there, the car broke down with a sickening crunch. 'Oh no,' said Godfrey, 'I'll never get the new job if I don't get there on time.'

'Don't worry,' said the driver. 'There's a garage round the corner. I'll nip off and fetch someone.'

What should Godfrey hear, a few minutes later, but the familiar sound of a toad croaking a funny little tune. Coming round the corner just after the croak, Jasper arrived.

They stared at each other. 'Who was it said that fixing cars was stupid, eh, and a waste of time?' said Jasper. 'If I'm so dim, why doesn't a clever chap like you fix it yourself?'

'I'm sorry, Jasper,' said the grasshopper. 'I've been stupid myself. I thought I was clever, but I wasn't clever enough to see that people like you, who can fix things, are just as important as people like me, who can do paperwork.'

So Jasper got to work fixing the car. 'You know,' he said, with his head somewhere inside the engine, clanking away with his spanners, 'I could never see the point of the kind of job you do, in an office, but I've been wrong too. Now my garage work has grown, I've got all sorts of paperwork to do with the business. I could do with a bit of advice.'

'Righto,' said Godfrey. 'I'm glad we're friends again.'

'So am I,' said the toad. 'Tell you what, let's celebrate your new job on Sunday afternoon with one of our old hopping races.'

Heavenly Father, help us never to look down on people who have different gifts from us, but to learn to value them.

HERCULES THE SECRET SERVICE FLEA

No one had ever seen a flea with a better suntan than Hercules. He got it when he went on secret missions to far-away countries — because Hercules was a Secret Service flea. It seemed to run in his family; he was always saying how his great-great-great-grandfather was one of the Flea Musketeers.

Once when he was back home, staying with his brother Archie, he hopped along one day to the school fête, though nobody knew. But all the time he was there, he used his Secret Service cunning to help them make money for the school. This is how he did it. Every time it looked as if the customers were good shots, then just as they went to throw, Hercules would give them a flea-bite, which made them jump, so they missed and lost their money, which meant all the more money for the school!

Now Hercules was back again and this time his cunning came in even more useful. His brother Archie used to work in a flea circus. One day, while Hercules was having a bit of a lie-in, in rushed his brother and shook him till he woke up.

'Whassup?' groaned Hercules, still half asleep.

'It's no good,' said Archie. 'I can't go to the circus and do my tightrope act today. I'm sure I'm going to fall off.'

'Don't be soppy,' said Hercules. 'You've been walking that

tightrope for years and you haven't once fallen off. What's up with you?'

'I feel all panicky today,' said Archie. 'I just can't face it. It's like the feeling you get if you've got to take an exam or a test, or if you've got to go on stage.'

'I'll tell you what I'll do,' said Hercules, with his cunning little flea brain ticking away. 'I'll hide up in the circus roof, and we'll tie a piece of string round you, so thin that the audience can't see it. Then if you start to wobble, I'll pull the string to get you straight again.'

Archie felt much better. He knew he couldn't go wrong now.

When the time came, the show was terrific, and Archie did his act better than ever. As soon as he'd finished, he rushed out to see his brother. 'You were marvellous, Hercules,' he said. 'That rope you held me up with was so thin I couldn't even see it myself.'

'I'm not surprised,' his brother replied. 'There wasn't any rope. You did it by yourself. I played a trick on you.'

'Why, you treacherous old Secret Service flea!' Archie cried. 'I could have killed myself.'

'Oh no you couldn't,' said Hercules. 'I knew you could do it, if you just stopped panicking. Everybody gets panicky once in a while; it's natural. But you've shown yourself now that you don't

need any secret rope to hold you up, and I bet you won't panic so easily again.'

Archie felt much happier after that, and went off cheerfully to work each day. As for Hercules, he just disappeared one morning. It must have been another Secret Service mission.

Heavenly Father, help us not to panic if we have to do something new. Help us not to be frightened of making a mistake.

IGNATIUS HAS A DREAM

E arly one Sunday morning Ignatius woke up, stretched and said to himself, 'Today I think I'll go to the service, and see what they get up to in church.' First he had a quick bite to eat. For the last few days he'd been chewing his way through an old story-book he had come across. He called it his breakfast serial.

Then he wriggled into his special mouse's four-legged pinstriped church trousers, and crept into church just in time to squeeze himself in between a very fat Cub and a very thin Brownie, so no one could see him.

He could hardly breathe with all the people there. And what with being squashed, and singing as loudly as he could, and having eaten one too many chapters for breakfast, he began to feel very peculiar. So he staggered out of the church, and tottered around the churchyard, unable to make his legs go straight.

All of a sudden a great, grey gravestone loomed up in front of him. As it came closer and closer he started to read the old writing on it: 'Sacred to the memory of Elizabeth Try, for thirty years schoolmistress of this parish, died eighteen –'

'Wham!' With a great crunching of nose, Ignatius walked right into the gravestone, and knocked himself out.

As he lay there, with his four legs, in his four-legged pinstriped church trousers, pointing to the sky, Ignatius had a dream. He dreamt he was in the old school. And there, at the far end of the old school hall, in an old-fashioned dress, sat Miss Elizabeth Try. The whole class – about fifty of them – sat in front of her on wooden benches, silently, because they could see the cane hanging on the wall behind her.

As Ignatius looked at her from the back of the hall, through the gaslight and the smoke from the coal fire, he heard her telling the story of Jesus when he went to the Temple and found that it was more like a market. He'd thrown their tables to the ground and said, 'My house shall be a house of prayer, not a robber's cave.'

'Now where have I heard that before?' thought Ignatius. 'I know, it was in church this morning, just before I started feeling funny . . .'

Then everything started going fuzzy and fading away, and suddenly he found himself back in the present again, lying on the grass in the churchyard. 'I must have walked right into that gravestone,' he groaned as he rubbed his sore nose, which had got bent sideways when he hit the stone. 'Oh well,' he pondered, as he crept back into the church, 'at least I'll be able to smell round corners now.' And that's just what he did.

As he went through the door, he was sure he could smell somebody's lunch. There, at the back of the church, was his friend Oliver the bat, who usually lived up the tower. In each of his leathery wings he had a packet of crisps, special bat crisps. One was cheese and ants flavour, the other was pigeons and vinegar. Oliver was munching and crunching as fast as he could.

'What do you think you're up to,' said Ignatius, 'sitting and eating your lunch here in church?'

'Why shouldn't I?' said the bat. 'It's cold up in that tower.'

Then Ignatius remembered his dream, and the story he'd heard Miss Try tell. 'I'll tell you why,' he said. 'It's because this isn't just any old building, it's what Jesus called a house of prayer. That means it's a special place for worshipping God and for saying your prayers, and for being quiet and thinking. Not for running around or chattering or eating your lunch.'

'Can't you say your prayers anywhere?' the bat muttered through the crumbs.

'Of course you can,' said Ignatius, 'But a church is a special place to help us think of God, and that's not so easy if there's a fat bat in the back seat deafening you with his lunch.'

'You know, mouse,' said the bat, 'you're a bit pompous sometimes, but you're right. What do you want me to do with my crisps, then?'

Ignatius was beginning to feel a bit peckish by now, so he said, 'Let's go outside and think about it. Maybe I can give you a hand.'

Heavenly Father, thank you for the churches where we worship you. Help us to remember that they are special places to remind us of you.

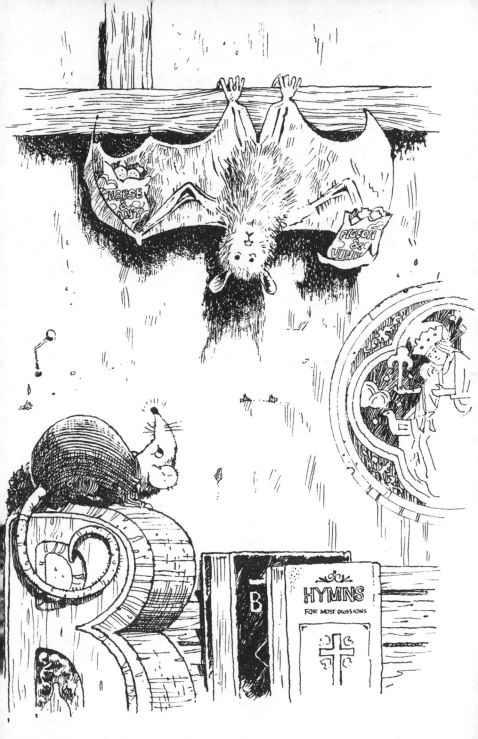

SUPERFROG

Down in the boiler room underneath the church, there used to live a frog called Sydney. Sydney's job was to check that the Vicar remembered to turn the boiler on to heat the church on Sundays. If he forgot, Sydney would hop through the Vicarage letter-box and flop on to the doormat, croaking away till the Vicar remembered.

One day Sydney was bored, so he hopped on a bus and went to see the new Superman film. He thought it would be terrific to be like that – one minute leading an ordinary life, the next minute able to do anything you like. 'That's what I'll be,' he said. 'I'm fed up with being boring old Sydney from the boiler room. From now on they can call me Superfrog!'

All the way home on the bus he puffed out his spotty green chest, looked the other passengers dead in the eye and croaked under his breath, 'Superfrog – I can do anything!'

When he got home to his boiler room, still croaking the magic word, 'Superfrog!', Sydney sat down and had a think. 'What shall I do, then? I know – I'll join the choir.'

So he went along to the choir practice that afternoon, really pleased with himself. At last he'd had the nerve to try something new. So they tested him. 'Sing this note,' said the choirmaster, and out came a great croak. 'Try this one instead.' Out came a huge honk. 'It's a froghorn,' said one of the choirboys.

Sydney tried and tried and tried, but it was no good.

As he flopped slowly down the steps to his boiler room, Sydney felt so ashamed. 'I'm no good,' he said. 'I'm useless,' as a great tear dribbled down his fat, froggy face.

Just at that moment, who should be going past the door but Ignatius, the church mouse, doing his rounds to check that the church was all right. When he heard the dismal dripping noise from Sydney's room, he tapped on the door and said, 'What's up, Sydney? Are you all right?'

'I was bored,' said Sydney as he opened the door, 'so I thought I'd try something new, and join the choir. But I was useless. I'm no good at anything.'

'Don't be daft,' said the mouse, 'just because you've been disappointed once. Everyone's good at something. Remember Harvey the octopus? He thought it was the end of the world when they wouldn't let him take up ballet dancing – until I told him to take up wrestling instead. What about you?'

'All I can do is hop,' said the frog, 'Hop and honk. What good's that? I –' Suddenly Sydney stopped talking. He'd caught sight of someone creeping out of the church, with what looked like the choir's silver trophy stuck up his jumper. Quick as a flash, with a mighty hop Sydney leaped down the burglar's neck and landed – inside the silver cup.

'Clang!' went the lid as the burglar slammed it down on top of the frog and ran off. What could Sydney do? He was trapped. He took a deep breath, inflated his spotty green chest as far as it would stretch, and let out a stupendous froghorn croak.

The burglar was terrified to find himself running along with his own burglar alarm. So he threw the trophy down, with Sydney still honking away inside, and ran away as fast as he could and was never seen again.

'Thank goodness,' said the choirmaster to Sydney that evening, 'that you can jump better than anyone else. And thank goodness you've got a voice like a froghorn after all. To show you how grateful we are, we're going to make you an honorary member of the choir. You can sit with us in church every Sunday, with a ruff round your neck and an enormous pile of music books – only don't try to sing.'

Sydney was overjoyed, and every single Sunday he's there, singing away silently. Though sometimes, as they listen to the choir, the people suspect that the odd frog-note slips out.

Heavenly Father, thank you for giving each of us different things to be good at. Help us, if we try the wrong thing first, not to give up.

NAPOLEON THE ENVIOUS EARWIG

In a cardboard box in the church porch lived an earwig called Napoleon. It was a very superior box, but Napoleon was miserable. Normally he'd jump out of his box as soon as the sun came up, scamper down to the station, wiggle into someone's ear and go up to London for the day. But now he hadn't been out for ages. The other animals noticed that Napoleon had lost his wiggle, and began to get worried.

After they hadn't seen Napoleon for a week, they sent round his particular friend, Archie the performing flea. He found Napoleon sitting on his cardboard box looking dreadful. 'What's wrong?' said Archie.

'I'm fed up,' Napoleon replied, 'fed up with being a scruffy earwig. Why can't I be something glamorous like a butterfly, or something clever like a bee? I wouldn't even mind being a flea like you. I just wish I wasn't an ordinary earwig.'

'Well,' said Archie, trying to be helpful, 'it's amazing what they can do these days. Why don't you go and see two or three of the other insects, and see what they think?'

'Okay, I'll give it a try,' said Napoleon, and scuttled off.

First he went to the bottom of the churchyard, looking for Walter the Worm. 'I'm thinking of becoming a worm,' said the earwig. 'Then I could worm away under the earth all day, safe and snug and out of the rain.'

'I shouldn't bother if I were you,' said Walter. 'You never see a soul, it's perishing cold down there, and if you're not careful someone sticks a fork through you. I always thought you were such a good earwig. It would be a shame for you to change.'

'I wonder,' thought Napoleon, and left.

Next he went down to the river to call on Neville the Newt. 'Well, this is an honour,' said the newt. 'What brings you here?'

'I'm fed up with being an earwig,' said Napoleon. 'I've always fancied being a newt, swimming around in the river all day instead of having to wiggle into people's dirty ears.'

'That's odd,' said Neville. 'I've often wished I could be an earwig. It's not much fun in the water, you know, day after day, trying to avoid the motor-boats and fishing lines and the great eels that want to swallow you up.'

Napoleon was surprised that Neville wanted to be like him. It cheered him up quite a lot. All the same, he thought he'd go and see one more friend, Plato the Centipede. He found Plato dozing peacefully in front of his fire, with his hundred feet nice and warm inside a hundred furry slippers.

'My goodness,' said Plato with a jump, 'It's you, Napoleon. I was just dreaming I was an earwig. It was such a nice dream. But what can I do for you?'

'I've come to ask your advice,' said Napoleon, 'About becoming a centipede. If I had a hundred legs like you, just think how I could dance! Or imagine playing football with a hundred legs, they'd never be able to tackle me!'

Plato lost his temper. 'For goodness' sake, Napoleon, you daft earwig, why are you wasting all your time wishing you were someone else? That's called envy, and it stops you enjoying being the person you are.'

That made Napoleon think. He remembered how Walter admired him, and how Neville the Newt had wished he was an earwig. Even old Plato dreamed about it. Maybe it wasn't so bad after all.

'There's one other thing,' said Plato. 'Unless insects like us learn not to be envious of other animals, we'll end up no better than anyone else. They're always wishing they were clever like so-and-so, or good-looking like so-and-so, or rich like so-and-so.'

As Plato was saying this, Napoleon felt a strange sensation coming over him. Sure enough, his wiggle was coming back. 'No time to lose!' he shouted as he rushed out of Plato's house and down to the station to catch a passing ear. Now he'd stopped wishing he was everyone else instead of the person he was, he'd begun to enjoy life again.

Heavenly Father, you have made each one of us special. Help us not to envy other people, but to enjoy being the person you have made us.

THE
WELLIGATOR

Just as it was getting dark one winter's afternoon, and the
churchyard was silent and full of fog, Ignatius the church
mouse decided to pop out of his nice warm room at the
church to fetch some snow. He had been getting his tea ready,
and fancied a snow sandwich. After his snow sandwich he was
looking forward to his favourite tea-time treat, toasted
hymnbooks, or as he called them, hymnburgers.

So out he went, into the fog and the snow. Suddenly, through
the gloom, he saw a huge black shape coming towards him out of
the fog. He turned to run back indoors, but with a crash the door
slammed before he could get there. He was alone in the
churchyard with the huge black shape, and it was getting nearer.

'Ignatius,' came a deep voice from the black shape. 'Ignatius,' it
repeated, getting closer and closer.

Ignatius was so frightened he couldn't move a step. 'Who –
who are you?' he said in a dry little whisper. And the great black
shape replied, 'I am the terrible man-eating boot of Old Malden.
In ancient times they called me the Welligator, and I have come
for you, Ignatius. Follow me.'

Ignatius was frozen to the spot with fear, motionless except for
a tiny icicle that trembled on the end of his nose. 'Come with me,'
said the Welligator again, 'or else you will suffer welligation.'

79

Ignatius had no idea what welligation was, but it sounded awful, so he forced himself to follow the Welligator, through the fog and the snow and in between the gravestones, into the furthest and gloomiest corner of the churchyard.

The Welligator looked down at Ignatius, who shivered and whimpered. 'What were you doing, Ignatius, yesterday at four o'clock?'

'I was . . . I was having my tea,' said the church mouse, 'Yes, I was just making a nice trifle out of bits of old candles.'

'Don't you *trifle* with me,' boomed the boot. 'Tell me again, what were you doing?'

'I was with Archie,' Ignatius confessed in a tiny voice, 'Archie the flea.'

'And what were you doing with Archie the flea?' said the Welligator.

'We were playing snowballs,' said the mouse.

'I know you were playing snowballs,' said the hollow voice. 'And who was inside the snowball?'

'Archie,' murmured Ignatius.

'And do you know how I know?' the man-eating boot went on. 'Because the snowball rolled into my sitting-room, and when it melted in front of the fire, there was poor Archie the flea, frozen and soaked to the skin and frightened and very, very miserable.'

'I didn't think,' said Ignatius. 'I never meant to hurt him. It was all a game, see.'

'It was a good game for you,' said the Welligator. 'But you didn't bother to think about Archie, did you? You were enjoying yourself, so you didn't notice he was scared to death. You're not a bad mouse, Ignatius, but you just don't think about other people's feelings. That's why I'm going to welligate you.'

The man-eating boot got up on top of the tallest gravestone, ready to welligate Ignatius. The mouse was so scared he couldn't move. Then things went dreadfully wrong for the Welligator. He slipped on some ice and fell off the gravestone, and out from inside the great long boot there rolled one of Ignatius' best friends, Harold the Mole.

Ignatius was thunderstruck. He didn't know whether to be glad that he wasn't going to be welligated after all, or angry with Harold for playing this trick on him. 'Why did you do this to me?' he shouted at the mole.

'It was to teach you a lesson, Ignatius,' the mole replied. 'Archie was so upset yesterday, that I decided to give you a scare, so that you knew what it felt like yourself.'

'I suppose you're right,' grumbled Ignatius. 'It seemed a good game at the time, but it was a bit cruel. Do you want some tea, Harold? I've just remembered that I came out here to get some snow for a snow sandwich.'

'I've got a better idea,' said the mole. 'Let's go round and have tea with Archie, and cheer him up.'

'Good idea,' said the mouse. 'Then I can tell him I'm sorry. And just in case he only gives us a tiny flea tea, I'll take some of my hymnburgers.'

Heavenly Father, help us to remember other people's feelings, and never to be cruel to those weaker than ourselves.

IT'S NOT MUCH FUN BEING A SLUG

SLUG NOOK
HAWKERS -
TINKERS - TAXMEN -
ANYONE WELCOME

U sually the grass in the churchyard is so long and jungly that nobody would notice a large flat stone in one corner. But it's not just a stone, it's somebody's home. Underneath it lives Solomon the Slug, and he calls his home Slug Nook.

He lives there because slugs like to stay where it's dark and damp. That's why you often find them when you turn over flat stones. The trouble is, nobody likes slugs. Not that there's anything wrong with being a slug. It's just that they're peculiar creatures, and every time somebody's doing the garden, and they turn over a flat stone and find a clammy slug underneath, they go 'Oooergh!' and drop it as fast as they can. It's not much fun being a slug.

This used to happen to poor old Solomon every time people came to do the churchyard which, luckily for him, wasn't as often as they should. At first Solomon would think, 'Oh good, here comes somebody. I don't get many visitors.' But as soon as they spotted him they would go 'Oooergh!' and drop him to the ground.

Solomon began to despair. 'I know I'm not much to look at,' he said to himself. 'But if only they'd bother to get to know me a bit, they'd find out I'm not half as bad as they think. Maybe I should just pack up my luggage' (or as he called it, 'my sluggage') 'and move away.' But he knew it would be just the same wherever he went.

Then one day, when he peeped out from underneath his flat stone, he noticed that there was a new gardener, an old chap called Len. Slowly Len weeded his way around the churchyard, until eventually he got to Solomon's gloomy corner, Slug Nook. Solomon knew what was coming. He gritted his teeth and shut his beady eyes as tight as he could, and waited for the worst.

Nothing happened. Slowly he opened first one beady eye, then the other, and gradually ungritted his teeth. There was Len the gardener, grinning down at him and chuckling, 'My goodness, I haven't seen such a great fat slug as you for ages.'

'What a cheek!' thought Solomon, though really he was pleased that someone was talking to him. They got chatting, and Solomon found himself saying all sorts of interesting things he didn't know he had in him, because nobody had ever bothered to listen before.

'But tell me,' he asked Len, 'why didn't you go 'Oooergh!' like everyone else, and shudder, and drop me to the ground?'

'Ah well, you see,' said the gardener, 'a few years ago, while I was weeding, I strained my back and had to go to hospital for a long time. The trouble was there was no room for me in the ordinary wards, so I had to go into the special Slug Unit. I was mad about this at the time, when I thought of all those horrible slugs I'd always heard about. But as I lay there day after day, with no one to talk to except the slugs, I found they weren't half as bad as I thought. The more I got to know them, the more I liked them. It's like some people. If you've never met anyone like them before, they give you the creeps, until you get to know them properly. Then you realise how daft you've been, and what you've been missing.'

Now, whenever Solomon hears the gardener coming, instead of gritting his teeth and clenching his beady eyes, he pokes his head out from under the stone to say hello. And Len comes along to do the churchyard more often then he used to, because he likes to see his sluggy little friend. But they'd never have been able to enjoy this if Len hadn't discovered that clammy slugs, like strange people, aren't half as bad as they seem, once you bother to get to know them.

Heavenly Father, forgive us when we shy away from people who are different from us. Help us to take the trouble to get to know them better.

SLUG NOOK
HAWKERS·
TINKERS· TAXMEN·
ANYONE WELCOME

SHERLOCK TO THE RESCUE

When the afternoons get darker and the ground gets frosty, Ignatius the church mouse gets very lazy. He curls up underneath the radiator in the vestry, and passes the day snoozing and toasting hymnbooks, to eat for his tea with shredded cassocks.

One afternoon he was busily looking for old books in the bottom of a cupboard, when he came across three old scraps of paper. 'That's handy,' he thought, 'an instant meal.' He picked up the nearest bit of old page, but just as he was about to pop it into his mouth, he saw something written on it. Ignatius wasn't a very good reader, so slowly he spelt out the two words. When he did, he froze to the spot.

In a frightened whisper he said, 'How did this bit of paper know I was going to eat it? Is this some sort of uncanny message?' There on the torn piece of paper he was about to chew up were the two mysterious words, 'inwardly digest'.

He snatched up the second scrap of paper. This had just one word on it. He could just make it out in the twilight. It simply said, 'embrace'.

Ignatius, who was a modest sort of mouse, blushed secretly under his fur. 'What sort of book is this?' he wondered. So he looked for another clue. He picked up the third piece of torn page. This one said, 'hold fast'. 'Peculiar,' he thought. 'First this looked like bits of a book on digesting, then on embracing. Now it looks like a book on wrestling. This is a bit too much for me. I need a detective . . .' So he sent for his cousin, a weasel called Sherlock.

When Sherlock arrived at last, Ignatius explained his three pieces of torn paper. 'Fascinating, my dear mouse,' said the detective as he puffed away at his detective's curly pipe. 'Let's take a closer look. We may find another clue.'

Sure enough, down a crack between the floorboards in the cupboard, he could just make out some more scraps of paper. So he fished into the enormous pocket of his enormous detective's overcoat, and pulled out a long pair of tweezers. With these tweezers he picked out – or as detectives say, extricated – four more bits of the page. On each of them there seemed to be another word. The first said HEARTH. The second EMTORE. The third ADMARKLE.

'What's an admarkle?' said the mouse. 'This is worse than ever.' Then up came the fourth scrap, which said ARNAND.

For a long time Sherlock was silent, just puffing his curly pipe in a weasely way, and shuffling the bits of paper around on the floor. Then without warning he let out a cry. 'Caramba!' – that's what great detectives say when they make a discovery. 'Do you see what's happened, Ignatius? Do you see what it says if we put these in a line? . . . HEAR THEM, TO READ, MARK, LEARN AND . . .'

'Well done, Sherlock!' said the mouse. 'But I still don't get it.'

'Patience, mouse,' said the furry sleuth. 'We must sleep on it.'

And sleep they did, right under the choir stalls. When morning came, they were woken by bells. 'Is it a fire?' said Sherlock, always suspicious.

'Of course not,' said the mouse. 'Today's Sunday, and the church service is about to begin. We're trapped.'

Just as he said that they saw, from underneath the seats, a procession of feet going by. First came a lot of brightly coloured

trainers. 'That's the choir,' Ignatius whispered. These were followed by a lot of enormous muddy black boots. 'That must be the servers,' he said. At the end there came a pair of old brown shoes that needed a polish. 'That's the Vicar,' Ignatius said.

The service began, and they listened as the Vicar read the special prayer for that Sunday:

'Blessed Lord, who caused all holy Scriptures to be written for our learning: help us so to hear them, to read, mark . . .' Sherlock and Ignatius sat bolt upright as they heard those words.

'. . . learn and inwardly digest them that, through patience, and the comfort of your holy word, we may embrace and for ever hold fast the blessed hope of everlasting life . . .'

The mouse and the weasel were so excited they didn't know what to do. At last they'd discovered what all those torn bits of paper were talking about, and Ignatius was jumping up and down on the spot, going, 'holy scriptures! holy scriptures! holy scriptures!'

As they hid there, they could hear the Vicar telling the people that this meant the Bible. He was saying how people should *hear* the Bible when they come to church, and as well as this should *read* it in their homes. They should *mark* it – that means remember it – and let it really sink in, the same as you *digest* your food. Because, he went on, if you want to be followers of Jesus, you've got to hang on to what he teaches in the Bible – you've got to *embrace* it and *hold fast*.

'Isn't he finished yet?' whispered Sherlock.

'Not long,' said the mouse, and as soon as the Vicar finished speaking, they slipped out. The mystery was solved. And they were so proud of those mysterious scraps of paper, they just couldn't bear to eat them for their tea.

Blessed Lord, who caused all holy Scriptures to be written for our learning: help us so to hear them, to read, mark, learn and inwardly digest them that, through patience, and the comfort of your holy word, we may embrace and for ever hold fast the hope of everlasting life, which you have given us in our Saviour Jesus Christ.

THE GRAND OLD MALDEN QUADRUPED'S MARATHON RACE

Everyone knew Arfa, the disgusting camel. Not so many people knew his nephew, who was a giraffe. In honour of his uncle they'd called him Girarfa. Nobody liked him much, because he always looked down on other people — which giraffes tend to do.

Early one morning, as Girarfa lay happily snoring in his special giraffe's bed, with its extension for long necks, something dropped through his letterbox with a loud plonk and woke him up. So he hobbled to the door, snuffling and coughing, and picked up a long envelope with the mayor's shield stamped on the top. As quickly as his sleepy hoofs could manage, he tore it open, and found an important-looking letter headed: Grand Old Malden Quadrupeds' Marathon Race. He grunted with a puzzled grunt, because he'd never heard of a quadruped before. He got out his dictionary and looked up the word, and found that a quadruped was any animal with four legs. He looked down and started counting his legs. 'One, two, three, four — jolly good, I must be a quadruped!' he decided.

The letter went on to say that there was going to be a four-legged race, and the prize was – to be mayor for the day. 'Wonderful,' thought Girarfa, 'I've always fancied myself as a mayor.' What he really fancied was having everyone admire him and think how important he was.

At long last the day of the race arrived, and all the quadrupeds were there. Crusty old Major Feele-Gloomy felt really left out, with only two legs. So he got together with Arfa's old friend Frank, and they borrowed a pantomime suit, and went disguised as a horse.

There was one competitor that not many people knew, a quiet, furry little creature called Eric. Eric the ferret. He was the sort of animal that people didn't notice, because he kept quietly to himself.

What they all had to do was to run as fast as they could from the school down to the main road at Plough Green. Then back to the church, up to the top of the tower, down again and back to the school.

As they lined up in the playground the crowd grew silent. In the mind of Girarfa there was only one thought. At all costs he must win, by fair means or foul. He had to be mayor for the day, and have everyone admire him.

There was a loud bang, a puff of smoke, the crowd roared, and they were off.

The first thing that happened was that Major Feele-Gloomy, who was the front legs of the horse, kept stamping with his great, black, shiny, military boots on the feet of poor Frank, who was the back legs. So over they tumbled, and every time they tried to get up, over they went again. That's what you get for pretending to be a quadruped.

As for the rest, it was neck and neck round the corner and along Church Road. Arfa the camel hadn't run anywhere for years, he was so disgustingly lazy. As soon as he reached the library he was so puffed out he collapsed on the bench, wheezing horribly, and try as he might, he just couldn't get up again. The rest of them raced on down to the main road, with Ignatius the church mouse in the lead. Suddenly he saw a steam-roller heading straight for him. What could he do? Quick as a flash, the nimble mouse jumped on a passing bus, and the next thing he knew – he was in Kingston. So Harold the Mole was the first to get to Plough Green. But he was so daft, and so gormless, that once he got there he forgot what to do next, so he burrowed under the earth.

That left just two of them racing back to the church, Girarfa and Eric the ferret. Girarfa tried every trick he could think of. He tried to barge Eric into the pond with a swing of his long neck. He tried to trip him up with his bony great shin. He even threw down banana skins left over from his breakfast. But Eric just kept going.

When they reached the church, Girarfa charged up the tower, shoving Eric to one side. But the ladders in the tower, sad to say, weren't all that safe. Just as Girarfa was getting near the top, he trod on a rotten step and with a mighty crash fell through.

'Help me, Eric,' he whimpered feebly, as he hung by his hoof tips over the great drop. 'I didn't mean to play all those tricks on

you. If you rescue me, I promise I'll race properly.' So Eric the ferret stopped, lowered his tail and pulled Girarfa up.

They didn't stop to speak, but slid down the ladders as fast as they could. Eric shot off, but came to a sudden and agonising stop when he found that the giraffe had tied his tail to the bottom of the ladder. 'Sorry you're too tied up to join me,' Girarfa cackled as he bolted on ahead to finish the marathon first. Eric felt like giving up, but slowly he untied his tail and jogged along to the school to complete the race.

Next day was the prizegiving, and all the quadrupeds were there. Right in the front row, with newly-polished hoofs and freshly-combed ears, was Girarfa. Up stood the mayor. 'First prize,' he announced in his important mayor's voice, 'in the Grand Old Malden Quadrupeds' Marathon Race goes,' and here Girarfa smiled an enormous, toothy smile, 'to Eric the ferret.'

A gasp ran through the hall. The mayor went on, 'The referee says that Girarfa only came first because he cheated. He wanted to win at all costs. Eric carried on despite all this, and without

trying to cheat back, so I declare that Eric the ferret, who was last, shall be first, and that Girarfa, who was first, shall be last. Because if I'm going to hand over as mayor for the day, it certainly won't be to someone I can't trust.'

Eric still remembers what a happy day he spent as mayor. And Girarfa still hasn't forgotten that painful lesson he learned, how the first can end up last, and the last first.

Heavenly Father, help us never to do wrong so that people will admire us. Help us to be people whom others can trust.

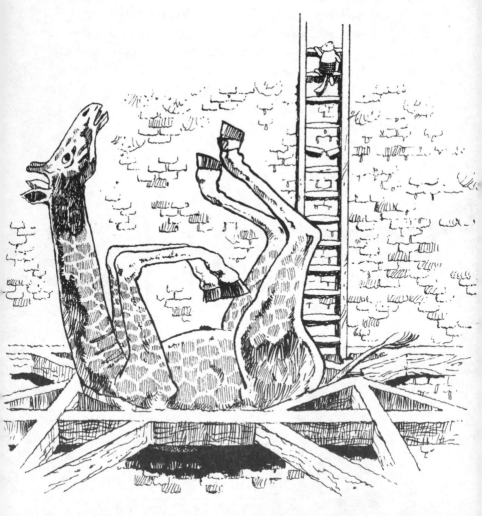